Published by Darf Children's Books
An imprint of Darf Publishers Ltd
277 West End Lane
West Hampstead
London
NW6 1QS

Dog, Cat and Mouse
By Bárður Oskarsson

Originally published as *Ein Hundur, ein Ketta og ein Mús*

Translated by Marita Thomsen
Edited by Beth Cox

Storyline and illustrations © 2004 Bárður Oskarsson

The moral right of the author has been asserted

All rights reserved

This book is sold subject to the condition that it shall not, by way of trade or otherwise, be lent, resold, hired out, or otherwise circulated without the publisher's prior consent in any form of binding or cover other than that in which it is published and without a similar condition, including this condition, being imposed on the subsequent purchaser.

A catalogue record of this book is available from the British Library.

Printed and bound in China by Imago

ISBN-13: 978-1-85077-321-4

www.darfpublishers.co.uk

BÁRÐUR OSKARSSON

DOG, CAT AND MOUSE

Mouse wandered around the kitchen.

She found a bit of cheese but she wasn't hungry.
She had already stolen some chicken off the table.

Mouse was bored.

There was a ball of wool on the floor for Cat to play with. But she didn't feel like playing.

Chasing Mouse was much more fun. A ball of wool doesn't run away.

Now they were all friends, even Dog, no one chased anyone anymore. And no one ran away.

Dog went for a walk, but stopped because he couldn't remember where he had planned on going. He just stood there in front of one of those things dogs are supposed to wee on.

I'm bored, I'm bored, I'm bored... he thought.

He was bored because he wasn't allowed to bark or chase Cat. Mouse had told Dog to behave.

That evening, Dog, Cat and Mouse sat in the living room. Nobody said anything. It was so boring.

Cat thought that it might be fun to chase Mouse or tease Dog.

Mouse thought that it might be fun to tease Cat.

Dog wasn't thinking anything, but he was thoroughly bored.

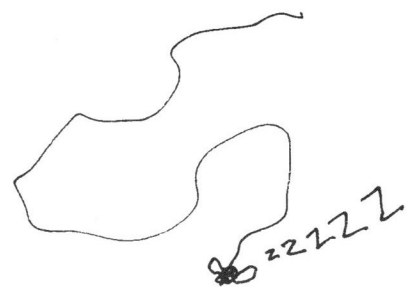

Everyone slept that night except Dog.
He was itching all over. He didn't have fleas,
he just really wanted to bark.

Dog tried hard to think, but his head tingled with
the effort.

He was angry with Cat because she wasn't afraid
of him any more.

WOOF WOOF WOOF!

WOOF WOOF WOOF!

Cat's heart leapt into her throat and she sprang up on top of the wardrobe.

It was good to bark again, thought Dog. And it was funny to see Cat so scared.

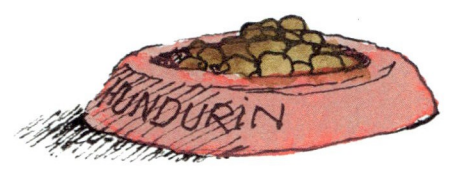

Cat was sure that it was Mouse who had told Dog to bark at her. It's what Mouse used to do before they all became friends.

Mouse was bored stiff and just staring into space when Cat jumped off the wardrobe and came flying towards her.

Next morning, Cat found a nice spot to rest.

Dog wanted to bark so badly that he was about to explode. And now, finally, the time had come.

He sneaked up behind Cat...

HIIIIIIISSSSSSSSSSSSSSSSSSS!!!

Mouse's tail nearly fell off she was so scared. She ran into her hole to hide and couldn't stop shaking.

Cat probably thinks I told Dog to bark at her, she thought. Stupid Dog. I'll show him.

That night none of them could get to sleep.
All three lay awake thinking.

Cat went to see Mouse and together they went to see Dog.

They all went into the living room to talk.
They had to figure out what had gone wrong.

Dog was watching TV when Mouse crept up behind him with a hammer. She aimed carefully and slammed it down on his tail.

BANG!!!

Dog yelped and howled. Then he hid in his basket and sulked.

He understood nothing.

"I was minding my own business, until Dog barked at me," said Cat.

"Then why did you chase me?" squeaked Mouse.

"You told Dog to bark at me!" said Cat.

"I did no such thing!" squeaked Mouse.

"And you took it out on my tail," sighed Dog.

"Yes, but that was because you started it!" squeaked Mouse.

"I couldn't help it, I was just itching to bark..." confessed Dog.

They chatted into the night.

This is nice, Mouse thought.